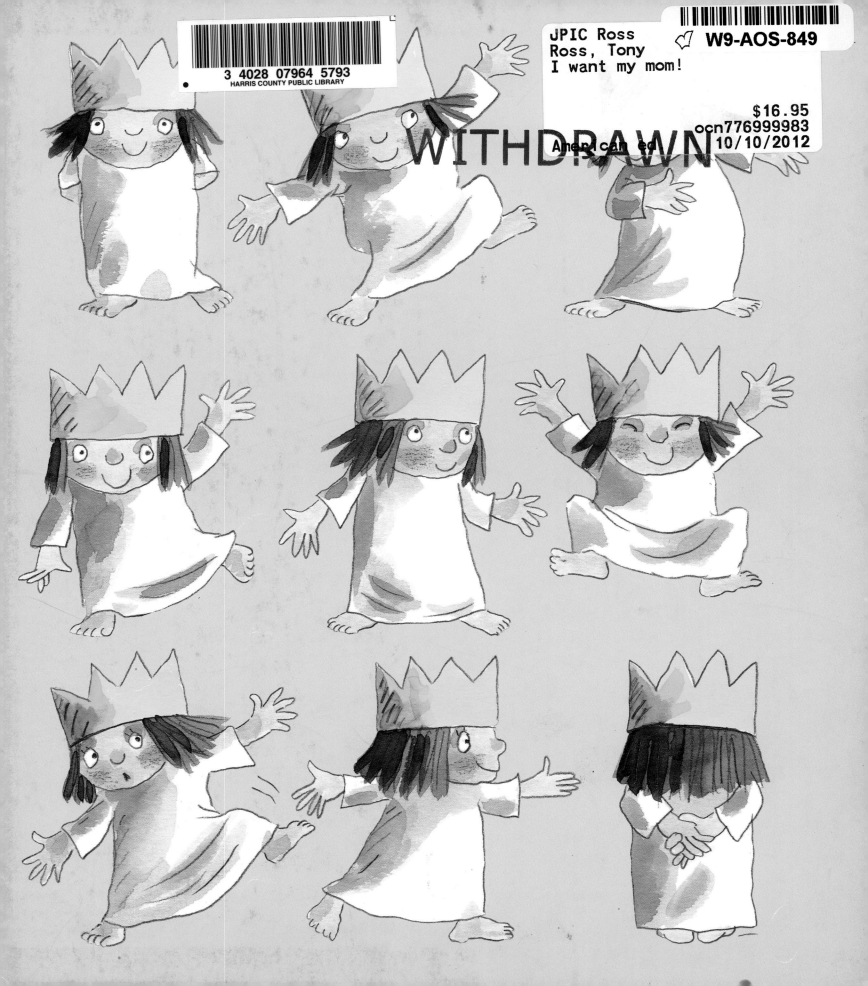

American edition published in 2012 by Andersen Press USA,

an imprint of Andersen Press Ltd.

www.andersenpressusa.com

First published in Great Britain in 2004 by Andersen Press Ltd., 20 Vauxhall Bridge Road, London SW1V 2SA.
Published in Australia by Random House Australia Pty., Level 3, 100 Pacific Highway, North Sydney, NSW 2060.

Distributed in the United States and Canada by

Lerner Publishing Group, Inc.

241 First Avenue North

Minneapolis, MN 55401 U.S.A.

www.lernerbooks.com

Color separated in Switzerland by Photolitho AG, Zürich.

Printed and bound in Singapore by Tien Wah Press.

Library of Congress Cataloging-in-Publication Data Available.

ISBN: 978–1–4677–0318–5

1 – TWP – 3/7/12

A Little Princess Story

I Want My Mom!

Tony Ross

Andersen Press USA

It was raining, and the Little Princess was busy with her painting when the awful thing happened . . .

. . . she knocked over her water and
spoiled the best painting she had ever done.

"Don't worry," said the Maid, "everything's OK!"
And she mopped up the mess.
"I WANT MY MOM!" yelled the Little Princess.

Mom held up the soggy picture.
"That's WONDERFUL!" she said. "A rainy day."
The Little Princess smiled.

When the rain stopped, she went outside to play on
the seesaw, and the terrible thing happened . . .
she banged her knee.

"There, there," said the Doctor. "That's OK now."
And she put some smelly stuff on it.
"I WANT MY MOM!" cried the Little Princess.

And Mom kissed the smelly knee better.
The Little Princess smiled.

That night, the Little Princess couldn't sleep because of the monster living under the bed.

The Little Princess packed her bag and began to cry.
"What's the MATTER?" said Mom.

"I DON'T WANT TO GO!" sobbed the Little Princess.
"I WANT TO STAY HERE WITH GILBERT AND YOU!"
"But Gilbert and I are coming with you," said Mom.

Back at the Royal Palace, the Queen
was chatting with the King.
"She's having a wonderful time," she said. Then . . .

"I WANT MY LITTLE PRINCESS!"

At last, Mom came with some thrilling news.
"The Little Duchess has invited you to a sleepover
tonight, with chips and a movie."

The Little Prince popped in to play anything at all.
And to stop the noise.
"I WANT MY MOM!" shrieked the Little Princess.

. . . but the movie was really funny,
and the chips were really good . . .
The Little Princess smiled.

At the Little Duchess's castle, the movie
started and Mom crept away.
"I WANT MY M . . ." began the Princess . . .

"There isn't a monster living under the bed," said Dad.
"Look!" But the Little Princess wouldn't dare.
"I WANT MY MOM!" she screamed.

"I'll read stories to you and the monster," said Mom.
The Little Princess smiled. And fell asleep.

"I HATE eggs!" said the Little Princess at breakfast.
"Eat up," said the Cook. "Eggs are awfully good for you."
"I WANT MY MOM!" howled the Little Princess.

"Oh, GOODY!" said Mom. "Dinosaur eggs.
I love those."
The Little Princess smiled. "Hey, save some for ME!"

All morning the Little Princess had to play by herself.
The Maid popped in to play Chutes and Ladders.
"I WANT MY MOM!" bawled the Little Princess.

The Admiral popped in to play boats.
"I WANT MY MOM!" hooted the Little Princess.

Other Little Princess Books